The Ghost and Lone Warrior

Dedicated to my three children, Matthew, Kristy-Marie and Joseph

©1991 C.J. Taylor

Published in Canada by Tundra Books,
Montreal, Quebec H3G 1R4

Published in the United States by Tundra Books
of Northern New York, Plattsburgh, N.Y. 12901

Distributed in France by Le Colporteur
Diffusion, 63110 Beaumont

Library of Congress Catalog Number: 91-65368

Canadian Cataloging in Publication Data:

Taylor, C.J. (Carrie J.), 1952-
    The Ghost and Lone Warrior
ISBN 0-88776-263-8

(Issued also in French under title:
Guerrier-Solitaire et le fantôme.
ISBN 0-88776-264-6)

    I. Title.

PS8589.A88173G46 1991   j398.2'089'973
C91-090241-0   PZ7.T39Gh 1991

The publisher has applied funds from its Canada
Council block grant for 1991 toward the editing
and production of this book.

Design by Michael Dias

Printed in Hong Kong by South China Printing
Co. Ltd.

The Ghost and Lone Warrior

An Arapaho Legend

C.J. Taylor

Tundra Books

Long ago in the days before horses, the people of the Plains had to go everywhere on foot, even when they hunted buffalo. Of all the animals, none was more precious. From the buffalo came food, clothing and covering for tipis. But sometimes no buffalo herds were seen on the grasslands. Then hunters had to walk far in search of smaller animals.

So it was that one bright autumn day Lone Warrior led a hunting party to the distant mountains. They carried food and spare moccasins for they did not know how far they would walk.

After two days they were halfway up the mountains when an accident occurred. As they crossed a stream Lone Warrior, the most surefooted of all of them, slid off a wet rock and hurt his ankle. Embarrassed, he picked himself up, pretended it didn't hurt and kept on walking. But by nightfall when he took off his moccasin, the pain was so bad he lay on the ground and prayed for sleep to forget his misery.

The next morning his ankle was swollen and hurt so much he could not walk. He told his friends to go on without him. "As soon as I can," he said, "I'll return to the village on my own."

His friends tried to make him comfortable. They built a lean-to against the mountainside, piled firewood within reach and left him with dry meat and berries to eat.

"We may not have to go far in the hunt," one of the women told him. "We'll look for you on our way back, in case you are still here."

Several days passed but Lone Warrior's ankle got no better. He made a crutch from a tree branch and was able to hop around and gather wood. But he would never be able to make it home.

His food ran out just as the weather turned bitterly cold. He kept a look out with his bow and arrow ready, but the cold had driven the birds and animals to take shelter.

Then the snow came. A blizzard raged all night long and almost covered his lean-to. The cold made him sleepy, but he knew he had to stay awake and keep the fire alive. He forced himself to dig in the ground under him for roots to chew on. Why had his friends not returned?

After the storm Lone Warrior dragged himself to the edge of a cliff.

On the plains below him was the most beautiful sight in the world.

A large herd of buffalo was digging through the snow for grass. Lone Warrior reached for his bow and arrow and took careful aim at the animal closest to him. He shot one arrow, then another, then another. The great beast bellowed and fell and the frightened herd moved off.

Lone Warrior felt a surge of strength. He climbed down the cliffside and crawled across the snow to the dead animal. Kneeling beside it, he looked up to the sky.

"Forgive me, Great Spirit of the Buffalo," he prayed. "I have killed so that I may have food and live. For this I am grateful and give thanks."

He used the buffalo skin to pull some meat back up the cliff. While waiting for the meat to cook, he stretched the skin over a rack and began to scrape it.

As darkness came on, Lone Warrior heard footsteps in the frozen snow. He stiffened with fear and clutched his knife tightly. It could not be his friends. They would have called out to him. What was it?

He did not have long to wait for an answer. Standing before him was a skeleton as terrifying as death.

"What do you want with me?" Lone Warrior asked, trying to hide his fear.

"First, you must feed me," the skeleton answered.

Forgetting his own hunger, Lone Warrior handed the visitor meat from the fire. The skeleton swallowed it before speaking.

"I am the ghost of your ancestor who was a great chief of your people. It was I who made you fall," he said. "And it was I who kept your ankle from getting well."

"But why?" Lone Warrior asked.

"If I had not stopped you, you would have been killed . . . like your friends. Killed by an enemy tribe."

Lone Warrior gasped. "My friends are dead? But if I had been with them I might have protected them."

The ghost shook his head. "They were caught in an ambush." Then, bending down, he touched Lone Warrior's ankle. "You can walk now. Follow me."

As if in a dream, Lone Warrior followed the ghost over the mountains through the star-filled night. When at last they stopped and looked down, he saw, in the distance, the tipis of his village.

"Why did you save me?" Lone Warrior asked.

"Your people need a strong leader. I believed you could be that leader, but I had to make sure. I had to see if you could keep your courage when you felt like giving up, if you could shoot straight in spite of your pain, if you could look at my face and not show fear."

Then, before his eyes, the ghost faded away and Lone Warrior started on the long journey home.

And so it was that Lone Warrior became chief of his tribe and his people were safe and prospered. Sometimes when he was tired, he liked to go alone back up to the mountain where the ghost had left him. Dressed in the skin of the buffalo he had killed that fateful day, and looking out across the plain to his village, he would feel the ghost with him, encouraging him.

The Arapaho

The Arapaho are famous as the great buffalo hunters of the
Plains and many of our stereotypes about the Indians seem to
be of them.

The picture of an Indian on horseback is so deeply ingrained in
the collective psyche of North Americans, it is hard to believe
that horses were only introduced to this continent by Spanish
explorers a few hundred years ago. Before then, the Indians,
especially the Plains Indians, lived a nomadic existence,
traveling great distances on foot as seen in this beautiful
Arapaho legend about courage and endurance.

As with most nomadic tribes, the Arapaho covered a great
area. The main settlements, however, were in southern
Wyoming and north-central Colorado, but the Gros Ventre (or
Big Belly) tribe, an offshoot of the Arapaho, inhabited parts of
southern Saskatchewan. The Arapaho's first contact with
Europeans occurred near the Black Hills of South Dakota.
Today, the 2,000 remaining Arapaho live primarily in
southeastern Wyoming and eastern Colorado. Besides being
remembered as "the elite of the horse Indians," they are
associated with the ceremony of the Sun Dance and known for
the symbolic designs of their beadwork. The legend of *The
Ghost and Lone Warrior* provides insight into the values that
the Arapaho felt their leaders must possess.

Sources of information: *Indians of the United States* by Clark
Wissler and *The Indians of Canada* by Diamond Jenness.

The Ghost and Lone Warrior is a retelling of the legend "The
Lame Warrior and the Skeleton" from *Tipi Tales of the
American Indian* by D. Brown.